Advance Praise for *Imaginary Ancestors*

Writing with the reinforcement of forty years of discipline, anger, passion and wit behind her, Madeline DeFrees offers us in this collection a complex and fractured portrait of her family history, at once comic and deeply tragic, but true, finally, in the way myths and jokes are true. And while DeFrees's poems acknowledge the luminous presence of Dickinson, Hopkins, Marianne Moore, and Bishop, no American poet writing today possesses the unfashionable courage, acetylene brilliance, and authenticity of this woman.

PAUL MARIANI

Not many writers today would dare claim Emily Dickinson as their grandmother, let alone end a wonderfully witty poem about an imaginary liaison between Dickinson and Gerard Manley Hopkins with the lines, "my Grandmother Dickinson, dyed in the clerical woof, / was warped for good. I am the living proof." But Madeline DeFrees does, and—brilliant, provocative poet that she is—gets away with every single one of the couplet's delicious double entendres, especially, and most emphatically, those which suggest that DeFrees's own "warping" is both "living" and "good."

PATRICIA GOEDICKE

Imaginary Ancestors is Madeline DeFrees's own *Genesis*, a book that makes a whole world and that makes her world whole. The landscape is linguistically lush; her "subjective geography," immense. DeFrees's imagination anoints the ancestors in the select society of this, her best book. A stunning achievement.

HANS OSTROM

Other Works by Madeline DeFrees

Poetry

From the Darkroom
When Sky Lets Go
Imaginary Ancestors (chapbook)
Magpie on the Gallows
The Light Station on Tillamook Rock

Prose

Springs of Silence
Later Thoughts from the Springs of Silence

Imaginary Ancestors

Imaginary Ancestors

Poems by

Madeline DeFrees

Broken Moon Press · Seattle

The following poems appeared in *Magpie on the Gallows*
(Copper Canyon Press, 1982): "Honesty," "The Bishops Bring
Tablets of Stone," "Burning Questions," "Grandmother Grant,"
"Ulysses S. Grant," "On My Father's Side," "Uncle Matt's Farm in
Cherry Grove," "The Widow," "What Makes or Breaks Them,"
"Gilbert of Sempringham," "Gerard Majella," "The Woman with
Fabled Hair," "Galileo's Case Reopened," "Sister Maria Celeste,
Galileo's Daughter, Writes to a Friend," "Emily Dickinson and
Gerard Manley Hopkins," "Ernst Barlach," and "Eminent
Victorians."

Thanks to the editors of the following publications in which some
of the new poems appeared: *The Southern California Anthology,
Fine Madness, Helicon Nine, Northwest Review, Pacific Review,*
and *Poetry USA*.

Printed in the United States of America.

ISBN 0-913089-14-1
Library of Congress Catalog Card Number: 90-83692

The publication of this book was supported, in part, by the King
County Arts Commission's Publication Project Award for 1990.

Broken Moon Press
Post Office Box 24585
Seattle, Washington 98124-0585 USA

For my Seattle network:
Andrea, Hans, Harry, Joan, Michele, and Pat

Contents

Acknowledgements

Thanks to Copper Canyon Press for permission to reprint poems from *Magpie on the Gallows* (1982); to Patricia Solon for help in production and to several correspondents and private line listeners who made the work less arduous.

Author's Note

Imaginary Ancestors began partly as an attempt to supply the missing links in my lineage on the side of an orphan mother; partly as a means to separate fact from fiction in her contradictory accounts of that heritage. The poems quickly extended to recover my own lost selves from the self imposed by thirty-eight years in the convent. As my personal landscape brightened—a process not always steady, but with the advances and retreats common to real life—the "Ancestors" grew to accommodate my literary and artistic influences and the points of connection with past lives and distant peoples. From the start I had envisioned a full-length collection. The poems published earlier should take on added resonance as they find their place in the more comprehensive picture.

Family Medicine

Stages of Family Life

My mother, the prima donna in the family
opera, conducted herself
like Callas. Stories she told were fabricated
from whole cloth, the fibers
synthetic. Not knowing your past could be
the shortest cut to a self-made
woman, Mother said, as she put her shoulder
to the wheel, believing she had
invented it.

        Through every crack in the door,
a grand entrance. For the least
innocent question, an oratorio. Clichés
drained from her hourglass,
precise as three-minute eggs, then turned
upside-down to start over. She thought of
the word as a bird in the hand
worth two in the aria. Each random complaint
provoked a recitative:

        starving Armenians
camped at the edge of our plates
waiting for handouts. Adrift in the city
the ghost of Horatio Alger
bound to win, decorated our mantelpiece
propped between ships coming in.

She filled the uncertain rest of her past with
trills and cadenzas. We remembered
our roles:

My brother, the bad one, pledged
to upstage her. My sister, the pretty one,
chose a doll for a diva. Our peace-
loving, book keeping father still
lived in the garden. And I, the reliable
smart one, trained my lorgnette
on the happiest scene, mere words no excuse
for the music in that burst
of elaborate dying.

Honesty

Money doesn't grow on trees, my mother said,
leaving out the dollar plant
dried in the Goldmarks' garden. All winter long,
it was my pocketbook,
thin membrane laminating seeds
that could be counted. Everyone else said Money
or Honesty. Mother rode trolleys,
waited for the stage.

That was the year her face flattened. Towards the cement
plant, the mint stretched
to the river. Crushed, it smelled like a letter
from Grandma, the one we never met.
Silver-haired and always
sending candy, she was my secret redeemer.
My brother said she hated the pope, Peter's bark
worse than Eve's famous bite.

We're not made of money, Mother said, and Grandma
shipped crates of oranges
that grow largely in California. The Book of Knowledge
showed *Lunaria*, tall with a silvery septum,
called it everlasting.
I wrote it all down, hidden in the chest
with my underwear. Summers at Rockaway, I collected
sand dollars.

           Moonwort, I said. Dipping my toes
in water I waited for incoming tide.

The Bishops Bring Tablets of Stone

Mother went to school in a cyclone cellar. She learned
not to fight long-haired cats,
not to interrupt or make noise, not to lie
or cry over nothing. Neighbor boys were bad. Mother
prayed and believed in Bishops—martyred Valentine,
St. Nick. Bring me a doll, she wrote in a newspaper
clipping. In the postscript, Don't
bring me a redheaded doll.

                                      All the stories had happy
endings. The barn wrapped in barbed wire
delivered to the next farm
earned a new cottage at the St. Louis Fair.
The paraplegic owner of the ax
hurled through an oak
took his show on the road to success, and Uncle Joe
looked away from the rattler in time.

                                       For once the parental
P. S. meant something. Our teacher said, Your letter
is a picture of you, tidy or not. What's important
belongs in the body. Mother's tissue-wrapped
curls in the tin box held
red glints. Auburn, Mother said, combing the evidence.
The bishop who rode a mule called her
strawberry blond. By the time I came on the scene
it had turned grey.

Burning Questions

Three times a week Mother set fire to the orphanage,
watched it burn to the ground.
If we poked among cold ashes we learned
records were destroyed. She cried over what we might
find. When the sun reappeared
she wrote letters. Tell me the true facts. You must
be hiding something. She thought
U. S. Grant had left her a fortune, too extravagant
for an orphan. The letter came back.
She tore up the Poles. What do they know? she said
watching eyes in the mirror
that were clearly Irish. They've mixed up the notes.

My father worked a bank that went broke. She took
to remodeling his side of the house. Dad
couldn't escape the perfect picture
frame. She turned him French overnight, beat the Dutch
out of his name, dabbling in white-collar crime,
the capital flourished in the middle.
That was before the Idaho Panhandle. It was great
on the Payette Bench, Mother said, looking
magisterial. The Blackfeet came into Brother Gene's
store and you had to watch them like Indians.
On our floor her wishes were law. For a minute
I nearly forgot she was Mother.

Grandmother Grant

Not the rejected lies of the New York Foundling
home, not the adoptive widow of two names,
one of devious spelling,
not the dogtag pinned to the plaid dress
for the train ride to Missouri, but the surname
worn like a shoulder brand
on the skin of the natural mother,
Grandmother Grant.

When I went in my black robes through the hot
streets of the city, a young nun
pale as the star I followed
led to the desk of a three-faced guardian. One
face called me Sister to my face. One was
motherly, "O my dear, I can't risk the wrong
information." One, older than the order, nervous,
bit the sentence off
on a fragment of Irish history.

I couldn't get past the gate. I recognized
the road I was on
led to heaven or hell. Either was barred,
date too early for the name,
A Closed File. I should tell my mother to come.
Back home in Oregon, sixty-nine, wanting to know,
not wanting to know, she waited.
I crossed the continent angry, three thousand
miles of featureless plain.

Mother, now that you're gone, I'm the same,
swaddled no more in the habit.
Whatever it is that drives us—bad blood,
the face in the unlighted window,
I'm bound to get it straight. If he knocked her down
in the stinking hold of a ship and raped her,
if she followed him out of the church
into the oldest garden under moonstone limbs
of the sycamore, it's too late
to cover her tracks.

       Whoever she was, whatever ties,
here is my claim. I need to come into my own.

On My Father's Side

Off the coast of Council Bluffs, Great Grandfather's
ocean liner went down. Years before
he sailed into the plan of God
Mother was already waving. She knew his ship
would come in, another miracle. I studied
the map of my head, painted the hull
orange. The mainsail was blue
over musical water. Nobody understood
how I fell heir to
the size of his hands like my father's.

All night in my head going down, the sea-keen
of his wake. I wrote his lament in the book
covered with envelope linings.
No one in this family can carry a tune, Mother said,
and I carried it to the attic. Safe there,
I threw my rag doll
a life preserver in the flood of infallible
pronouncements. My father's father's father's voice
rolled like the sea
through my father's impossible speech.

Uncle Matt's Farm in Cherry Grove

The uncle not really an uncle, Mother's second-
fiddle makeshift dad, wore the same coat
to church and in the garden. His money wouldn't
stretch. He couldn't keep his head
above water, the uncle who had
to be taken away. Bill collectors trailed him
in the hospital: rec room, bathroom,

bed. Near a small water wheel on Uncle Matt's farm
I saw my first muskrat. I was eight. I stood
very still while the animal
went under water. Uncle Matt was better, but his coat
was too big. I was waiting for the cousin
not really a cousin I might marry later, who lived
in our house and played our piano.

                                    He brought
orchestras into our living room. When he was gone
I carried his postcards in my pocket, slept with them
under my pillow. Would he come home? Digging
shrubs in the hospital dirt, Uncle Matt found
himself. What he lost, I could lose.
That part made it hurt. It was everything.

The cards were beginning to crack and tear. I took
them and my books into the Cherry Grove
sun, tracking the print with a finger, following one
through the mud. I was glad and scared. I can still
bring back the pale whiskery scramble. The brown
coat, red where the frayed
light fell and the natural musk.

The Widow

There was a self-made widow far back in the trees,
wore black even in summer, black
to her unsung bridal. Knelt for the cross of ash
on lip and forehead, ash
sifting down to the covered breast, the ritual
giving of palm.

                      That too eager martyrdom of wishes
sent before the blood, drained color
from the skin, leaving the breakable face
in the circular window. Truth
supported her, that ingrown toenail of the ordinary
saint walking on ground glass.

                      Windows of unreal space,
her sanctuary opened on the widow's walk of miners;
everything learned by rote rejected, everything
but the guilt. See how the palm
droops toward wilting lids, eyes rolled
to her lord or her lord's envoy,

                      halo conjured
from heavy air. Eyes cast modestly down,
the statuesque pose of eyes on a plate.
Never the clear gaze of the whole woman, always
sackcloth and lamentation,
the penitent's crown.

                      Today October haze
crowns the mountain, leaves crack underfoot, shock
tilting the earth's crust. Black glasses I wear
peer through her eyes as I kick
the leaves aside and sing for the widow glass.
She falls at my feet breaking the cold surface,
ash floating on air the dust settles.

Saintly Patrons

What Makes or Breaks Them

Greatness was something in the bones: it meant
a kind of two-way stretch, sinner and saint
cut from the same bright cloth.
My namesake, Mary Magdalen, a case in point. These
were the better sort, and some
had gone the wrong way first as I had not.

From the convent cell where I fasted and prayed,
I studied the fine print of those loose
women who strayed door-to-door,
desert-to-desert, ending always in the right camp.
That was the mammoth risk, swung prehensile
over the Garden Wall.

I would have been less categorical, but in between
lay namby-pamby. I thought of the foreign
missions. Japan: sitting cross-legged
through ceremonial teas and formal addresses, barely
moving a muscle. Eating seaweed cookies, taste
of rotten fish.

       In South Africa, a slash from crotch
to gullet, not quite my dish, either. Vague
tales of babies delivered, learning to speak Sosuto,
the woman whose tumor weighed fifty pounds. I parried
the rain of stones on Christian heads
old men bought from the witch doctor.

                                                  Stuck on prim
rosepaths, I cultivated lilies and languors for all
they were worth. Sometimes a rift
in the wall, crack in the door, brought in the virile
drift of ocean, its salty crash. Carried away
by Margaret of Cortona's role, my head swam
to meet that model penitent.

                                     Like her, my days
and nights were spent in tears—without a checkered
heaven to make them credible. Mornings, chapel windows
wide, thermostat on 50, St. Mary of Egypt's desert
sizzled comfort. Her diet was inedible;
sunburn-cloak, less than modest. I admired
her walk on water, preferred

                                        alligator pears to lentils
at the farewell banquet, agreed the lion digging
her grave would be a smash on the dust jacket. Still,
I didn't have the nerve to back it up. The raves
rang false: early rapture, crocodile tears—most of all,
the late affair with Scripture—wouldn't wash.
The woman couldn't write or read.

Clare of Assisi

Far ahead, we could already make out the bishop
on his way to our parish. Confirmation
time, time to choose one more saint
to protect us. I settled on *Colette,* but my
copycat friends followed suit, and those
carbon Colettes were too common.

                                          In secret
I transferred to *Clare,* pleased to honor
Clarence, my father: a name so clear
it signalled the onset of trumpets or Shakespeare's
flourish of hautboys, the clarion
sweetly confused in my mind with a carillon.

Then it was bells followed me everywhere, chimed
through the night-deep waters of
drowned cathedrals. Bells transmuted to birds
singing *Poor Clare, Poor Clare,* all through
the early light where the maiden walked
barefoot, spirit-sister to Francis, *Francis,*
my own bad brother's second of three
given names.

                              Clare ran away when they
wanted her married, changed at the church door
her sumptuous clothing for sackcloth
and, shorn of her hair, clung to the altar when
relatives came to drag her away. Clare
carried the day.

I carried her name but shrank
from the unwashed poor. I wanted them
shaven and showered with clean underwear. I
wanted them nice. At the New York Passport
Agency, I took the official
advice: *Drop everything but the Madeline.*
You'll save yourself

        all kinds of trouble. I
saved myself. Chopped off the *Mary,*
axed out the *Clare,* forgot about burlap and
beggars, let go of the altar. Assisi was a lot
like Camelot, as hard to forget.
With ocean and lake everywhere, I still
hear those bells under water.

Gilbert of Sempringham

Plain Gilbert to me, who wore with a heavy veil
the luckless name let down by a bishop
on my shorn head: "Henceforth you will be known as
Gilbert," the same given first
to a New York nun in an extant grave, who wrote
Our Nation's Builders, stacked
in the classroom cupboard.

The fifth grade clapped when I came. "Sister, did you
write this book?" their eyes bigger than the words
inside. I shook my head, refusing to claim
that honor, showed them the dictionary. The books
never wore out, their blocks
longer than chapters I learned to translate
a paragraph at a time.

Gilbert, my saint, if I had you my own, always
in the shadow of the great. "The real
Sister Gilbert was a saint, was she your aunt?"
Should I tell them I hated the murky lines? They quoted
her life of the foundress, room gone in the haze
of Mother Mary Rose, I tried
and the fifth grade was right.

O my English patron, believe I drew water from your
twelfth-century springs.
Only the Gilbertines survived, your order
of nuns, not the men

you gave them as masters; those and the crumbs
you scraped from refectory tables,
pledged to discourage waste.

I gave you the frugal ways of my imitative life.
How could I follow you, founder,
lost as I was with my foundling mother, starved
ghost of my convert father,
under a shroud at sixteen in all weathers, white
body lost in heat,
not even my name new-borne?

Gerard Majella

Among ancestral saints Gerard Majella, tailor's
apprentice, took first place as well as second.
He could bilocate, served a bad-tempered
bishop. I wore his medal with the other
over my heart—Benedict,
saint of expectant mothers—under the black serge
cape, the reefs and shoals
of that halting voyage.

                       Gerard, they said you must not
attract notice, confined your wonders to such
as monks approved. I used to watch that careless
workman hang in clear air under the scaffold
before the cumbersome machinery
moved. Traitor to my land, I wanted words to come
to term more than I wanted God, clung to your blessing
hand, straddled the Great Divide,
cheered when you came from your ghostly father.

                             Stitching
unstitching hours in mid-air, the lines seemed a decade's
thought. They wound the dim passage in black
sleeves of Latin that sing to me yet.
You put the platform back under awkward feet
as I passed, rich, through the needle's eye, balance
restored and my mind
clear as the head in another planet,
eyes on the right ground.

The Woman with Fabled Hair

In the life to come I unravel and let down
the extravagant bolt of hair,
the braids of a saint caught in silk
all the days I remember. Cut free of the tin box
the future crown is always mine. Repeated
shocks of auburn, shades of my mother's
upswept hair when she ran away
with the man who would fade to my father.

I am waiting for him to come again, the simple
man in elaborate disguise, wearing his
bones like a prophet. When enough time has been
lost, her hair will fall to my shoulder.
Dense folds released from the veil, this past
woman's glory recovered
brings back the forgotten blend, lilac and
amber, cypress and plum.

The man will look into my eyes when I come
for the girl in the glass, the one to be
lifted down from the wall where she hangs
in the white dress, the too-short curls. "We have
plenty of time," taking the girl's right hand.
"We have from now on," stroking the nails
she tried to press down, kissing them. He won't mind
that her teeth are set far apart,

believing that passionate sign. *Don't be afraid*,
and the brain in its time carries her
over the doorstep, engraved words to a bride.
These forevers that keep
disappearing, bureau drawers of a life
that threatens to move us out. The body
meets the animal it ran from: dark bush
parted in the night, wet fur, the cave lighted
by the eyes of lynx, my own
dense longing.

Seven Questions for Catherine-at-the-Wheel

Who could refuse the saint who gave her name
to a firecracker? A rose window? Did one
wheel or four fall apart to save you? What sign
made the emperor run away in shame?
Did convertible heathens burn the same
as canticle Christians, bodies well-done
and faces chromium, unlike our own,
revving it up in perennial flame?

Are my burning questions asked in good faith,
whose hands for half a century escaped
the wheel? Why am I engineered to pray
aloud to myself, mechanic friend of Death
the Demon, whose black right hand I gripped
two decades past, driving my first Chevrolet?

Teresa of Avila

Many Theresas have been born who found for themselves no epic life . . .
GEORGE ELIOT, Prologue to *Middlemarch*

Part of her soul ran deeper than still waters,
extension of intellect
rich as the color and texture
brocade embodies. The rest rang clearer than
clarinets, a confident line
where the trill eddies into the melody.
I loved her best because she believed the mind

mattered. When I walked the streets of my home-
town, egghead in a circus, I felt like a
freak, the high-wire act of my brain
treading a tenuous line towards
conclusion. Everyone waited for my regrettable
leap—teachers too—my questions a nuisance,
some devil always at work in that

towering pride. This woman's wit, a revelation
come down on my side, gave me
courage. *It is no light cross*, she writes, *to
submit our intelligence to someone who
hasn't very much himself.* Her solution: don't
do it. This saint who called the piercing
of her heart "exchange of courtesies between

the soul and God" inspired Bernini's sculpture.
The *Ecstasy* shows the ambiguous
line between orgasm and rapture, the wounding
cherub closer to Cupid, perhaps, than
we'd like. Teresa's beside herself as the saying
goes, at a time when *ecstasy* means out of
control, the history of hysteria. Some of us know

another kind of displacement: the self divided.
Plato draws an irrational line down
the middle: body on one side,
mind on the other, a purely logical distinction.
Such neat operations deserve more
delicate scalpels. Bernini's marble opens a
door to belief: in sex or religion, as if

one excluded the other, the views of the viewer
surprised in relief. Teresa—woman and saint—
the turbulent flow of your
habit is music. Heart so grateful you said, *I can
be bribed with a sardine,* some days
these days I understand what you mean: those
first moments after we dive to the bottom
discover the rapture of the deep.

Historic Figures

Arthur Strangeways

His name stands first on a chart of my father's
clan in this country. Arthur Strangeways
arrived in the mail from a man at Cornell who'd
plucked my name from a dust jacket. *Don't
write back,* my mother said. She knew
from the *Reader's Digest* this was a scam.
Of course I wrote back because that's the way
I am—contrary as Mary, Mary. My first name
really fit, which may be the reason
I didn't go by it. *He'll send you a bill,* Mother
said. I tried to stay cool. *OK
then, I'll pay it.*

          When I squinched my eyes at
the xeroxed sheet, four generations from the
first Defrees, Arthur floated in a dead white
space. No date at all. No country, town, state.
He could be anyone I wanted. Pretty soon
I could tell, Arthur's eyes were hazel. Through
the fine script, his 17th-century
face unblurred. Dubbed over my mother's voice,
it was Arthur's I heard. As a child, I'd told her
Dad had the lightest eyes in our brown-
eyed family of five. *Hazel,* Mother said. *Your
father's eyes are hazel.*

          Name nearly as good
as Andrew Marvell's, Arthur could have
lived in the same era. For all I knew they were
cousins: Arthur and Andrew, the strange and
the marvellous. My link to the Metaphysicals.

The flip side of these fantasies
veered towards the violent ward. There was that
not-quite-uncle who cracked up in the depression.
My mother's mood swings. And always,
my teachers' warnings to get more fresh air,
take a break from the books and
my "nervous constitution."

                             My father's strange
ways began to come clear as I plumbed
the paternal line: those days when my mother
boarded a bus for Portland, not taking us
to shop or consult a doctor. The three-layer
Chocolate Never-Fail Cake, uncut
in its plastic holder, sat on the counter. Intact
on the icebox shelf, the beef roast
meant for our dinner. All over the kitchen,
Mother's copious notes on provision. *Enough to
feed an army for a month*, my father
said, breaking out the loaf

                           for bread-and-milk,
served in glasses with sugar. He diced
the bread precisely, gave spoons
to my sister and me, sat down silent with us in
the marvellous dusk, as we savored our
strange Arthurian supper, perfectly happy.

Ulysses S. Grant (1822–1885)

The Treasury voted nine to one against your ordinary
chin, though you cut mustache
and beard to sit for the profile photo. With Liberty,
that noble woman, your dreams of fame were half
dollars, the silver part
aristocrat like millionaires of Boston Common,
the homespun sage of almanacs, obverse
eagles and bells.

           More than the rest, Mother believed
blood tells but wouldn't say what. She
claimed you—with or beyond reason—saving the pencilled
Mary Grant pinned to the front of her faded plaid
like an heirloom. I read available
histories, imagined Army tanks of social disease
rolling down, a plague on my doorstep. Expected my mind
to go off, the slow tongue
fused by drink and vague neglect.

           Under the West Point
manners and epaulets, beat the timid heart of a store-
keeper. I joined your campaign against migraine,
kissed your clay feet warm, hung over
the bedpost, head split clean as rails of your honeymoon
cabin. In Mother's kodak, Dad stands in knee-length
coat, starched shirt and hat, one hand on a post,
stunned by the history he's come into.

                                        On the back
in Mother's cursive hand, a legend of relationship
to Julia Dent, Grant's First Lady.
It makes no sense without a double tie, adoptive
mother and real in league
to right some kinsman's wild throw. *Little pitchers
have big ears,* Mother says, and so
the story closes. I watch the smoke from a president's
quota—20 cigars a day—ticket

                                        to cancer of the throat
and memoirs written, dying. A family man to the end
he sold his life for wife and children. Even now
the overheard alarms. Mother died of a perfect heart
tracking invented lives through the land, the record
always partial. I look for her nine-years' grave
through a light sifting of snow, travel cold
as she lies without a coat of arms.

Galileo's Case Reopened (1564–1642)

Lie still, son Galileo, while we crack
the seal, undo the nails and let the bronze
repeal of history correct your bones.
And what's three hundred years, the long trajec-
tories of moons, their lines criss-crossing like
a pinball game? Believe me, no one wins
without a slight distortion of the lens
changing the curve of inference and luck.

Timely as rockets bursting on the mind's
black earth, I plant the fleurs-de-lis of kings
over your grave to mark the faithful skull.
Inside the socket where the globe unwinds,
the shaken bell of every iris rings,
your brain flowers like a solar model.

Sister Maria Celeste, Galileo's Daughter, Writes to a Friend

Again I am at sea. If this be faith, it is not
the faith I bargained for
when I gave that troubled half-life over; the slow
sidereal day in trade for a guarantee
the drift persuades me to consider.

                       This morning
lifting the shipboard cup from my lips into the hands
of my judges, the cheap wine cloying my tongue,
I see the rift clearly. Nothing—not words, the unlikely
notice of scholars, not the face
set towards a cruciform sun; least of all, the ritual
meant to distract us—eases this passage.

                           I have
bargained everything away for the slow word, hard
as science, for an uncertain page
in the text of the future. Have taken in vain
the name of God's mother, coupled it with foreshortened
heaven. This is my home
voyage, too fast to be wasted in anger.

                          Call me a vessel
come in from the peaks and valleys written in water.
Blot out my name. Moored to my own
tilted deck, I ride, I am riding
the battered hulk to the ocean floor.

Horatio Alger (*1834–1899*)

Books were the air I breathed, curled in the Morris
chair with the Wizard of Oz or thousands of leagues
undersea—a place I could never go without
Jules Verne. So little time. So much to learn.
Too many distractions. *Set the table.*
Dust the woodwork. Get some fresh air. Go to
the store. Time for bed. Mother hid books
on top of the kitchen cupboard.

                       A Carnegie
uncovered in our family tree would keep me in books
indefinitely. More books than Mother could
whisk out of sight. When my brother brought home
from his paper route a ton of Horatio Alger, I read
them aloud, night after night. *Ragged Dick.*
Adrift in New York. Tom the Bootblack. Fame
and Fortune. One story

                           repeated 119 times. Andrew
Carnegie's autobiography repeats it again.
No wonder I recognize
those long-dead volumes brought from the library
mausoleum. Once upon a time I could breathe
life into their creaky lungs. Candidates for
the oxygen tent, they spoke in
borrowed tongues

                    like the lines of my early poems.
Fashioned of Mother's platitudes
mixed with rhyme, meter, and Horatio Alger, once

removed, hints of the pure sublime
sneaked into newspaper columns: a long dream of
fame—never a dream of fortune. *Your poem
in the Oregon Journal helped me in my trouble.* This
in a shaky hand from a man

                          who sent me a dollar
bill. The poem was "Sympathy." I was
thirteen. Six lines in rhymed couplets. I can
recite them still. Ragged Dick
had nothing on me. This had to be The Little League
American Dream. Like Author Unknown,
like Anonymous, I had arrived,
was secretly famous.

Andrew Carnegie Compared to the Air
We Breathe (1835–1919)

Because his parents believed in pets, Andrew kept
rabbits, his first business venture. Recruited
playmates to gather clover & dandelions.
The name of a boy who persevered for a season was
given to a rabbit. Years later on a train,
Andrew met a tycoon who confided, *I was one of
the rabbit boys.*

                In Allegheny City, he made one-
dollar-twenty a week as bobbin-boy in a cotton
factory. Tending the boiler kept him awake
after dark. He sat up in bed
turning and twisting gauges. Too little steam
made the workers complain. Too much, and
the boiler exploded.

                 Transferred to accounts, he
still had to bathe the bobbins in oil.
The smell made him gag. He crossed the river into
Pittsburgh, worked as messenger-boy
for a telegraph company, *lifted,* he said, . . . *into
paradise . . . with newspapers, pens,
pencils and sunshine about me.*

                Free enterprise
inhaled at 13 lent incentive. Over the whole
country—a de la Renta perfume—the crisp
green smell of money. At 30, resigned from

the railway, he vowed never again
to work for a salary. From bobbin-boy to a man
of steel, his story is true

                     Horatio Alger. His
Gospel of Wealth, like the Parable of the Talents,
asks a return on investment. The talents
are said to be coins—one, two, or five—what each
servant does best. The charge: not to hoard
but give back with interest. This poem for instance,
dead or alive, its own reward.

The Sleepwalkers' Dialogue*

Stage Manager:
> Out of the shadows, over the years, the miles,
> these characters walk in their
> paradoxical sleep, talk to themselves, talk
> to and about one another.

Galileo Galilei:
> [*To Andrew Carnegie*] Your Hero Fund "... for
> families of those who perish ... to serve
> and save their fellows." Surely, I've done
> that. I discovered the four
> moons of Jupiter. Joined 80 stars to nine
> in the belt and sword of Orion ...
> protected Venice from invasion by sea.

Carnegie:
> Ah yes! A city seated on a harbor cannot be
> hidden. You increased the power of
> the naked eye, but did the Venetian Senate
> not double your pay for that? My Fund
> had the common man in mind, the unsung hero ...

Galileo:
> But consider my unjust punishment! My *Dialogue*
> forbidden. The "formal prison," albeit served
> in a villa and a palace. My religious
> sentence: to repeat weekly for three years
> the seven penitential psalms ...

---

* Italic passages are drawn directly from recorded words of the speaker
(e.g., from Carnegie's *Autobiography*), or from a contemporary.

Carnegie:

How well I recall those spirit balms! *One of
the trials of my boy's life was
committing to memory two double verses . . . to
recite daily.* On a slow walk to school
I could master the task and shine in the first
lesson. Thirty minutes later, I'd forgotten
everything, not being impressed.
But didn't your Carmelite daughter, Sister
Maria Celeste, serve this part of your sentence?

Galileo:

Duly approved by the hierarchy . . . my time—of more
value than hers—better spent in science.
I'd hoped that your grants were retroactive like
the Pope's vindication . . .

Carnegie:

Take this copy of my *Gospel of Wealth.* You may
find something useful. And remember:
A sunny disposition is worth more than a fortune.

Galileo:

[*Exits left*] What an idiot! He begins to sound
like Dale.

Carnegie:

> What a thoroughly unpleasant fellow! All rant
> and rail, but not my company!
> Now General Grant would never put on such airs.
> *I never heard Grant use a long or grand*
> *word or make any attempt at "manner."*
> *When he had nothing to say, he said*
> *nothing.*

Sister Maria Celeste:

> [*Enters right*] Ulysses the Silent, they called
> him. I'm good at that, too. The Carmelite
> vocation. My father, alas! was
> never contemplative, his sojourn among stars
> notwithstanding.

Stage Manager:

> I see what Grant's friend, John Burroughs,
> meant: *he walks with men of money now.*
> Success in war, another version of Horatio Alger's
> American Dream.

Galileo:

> [*A voice from the wings*] Horatio Alger, that
> despicable mealy-mouth!
> When he had nothing to say, he
> preached a sermon.

Ulysses S. Grant:

> [*Emerging from ambush*] Andrew! There's someone
> I'd like you to meet. He'll put an end
> to these diarists who give the record to Grant:
> *Odysseus knows how to keep his own*
> *counsel and shuts up, close as an oyster.* You
> must have had enough of the Italian's
> fish-wife talk. Andrew, Arthur Strangeways.

Arthur Strangeways:

> [*Silence*]

Sister Maria Celeste:

> Nothing to say, Strangeways? Not even an oral
> history? I seem to have found my speech
> after long silence . . . Perhaps we *need* Horatio
> to keep the dialogue flowing.

Horatio Alger:

> [*Enters from right*] You were speaking of
> heroes? Twice on my way to enlist
> I broke my arm and suffered a sore rejection.
> Thereafter, I served my country as recruiter
> and later, drilled a detachment of
> Cambridge boys in military arts. One, a lad
> of 15 named Wilbur Cross,

I was paid to tutor
in French and Greek. He had no talent
for language, so I taught him what he would
learn: to march and salute smartly,
to carry a stick like an authentic
weapon. *My* gun was a violin bow, befitting
my loftier station.

All went well until Wilbur's
father tested him on French verbs and promptly
discharged me. Next, he withdrew his son—
a private at the time—just when I'd planned to
promote him. Wilbur ran away to the army.
He wrote me a letter. Johnny Popetetzky was
there. They were eager

for battle, hoping not to
get lice and surrender their hair. They sent me
salutes. You see what the right
influence can do. You see how I served my country.

Grant:

"Who serves his country well has no need of
ancestors."—Voltaire

Galileo:

"I can trace my ancestry back to a[n] . . . atomic
globule. Consequently, my family pride is
something in-conceivable. I can't help it! I was
born sneering."—W. S. Gilbert

Alger:

> "Our ancestors are very good kind of folks, but
> they are the last people I should choose to
> have a visiting acquaintance with."—James Madison

Sister Maria Celeste:

> "People will not look forward to posterity who
> never look backward to their ancestors."—Edmund
> Burke

Strangeways:

> "My family history begins with me, but yours
> ends with you."—Plutarch

Galileo:

> "[The Great Father's] presence here . . . is an insult
> to the spirits of our ancestors."—Red Cloud

Carnegie:

> "It is indeed desirable to be well descended,
> but the glory belongs to our ancestors."—Plutarch
> again!

Grant:

> This war of quotations grows tiresome. *Let us have
> peace.*—Presidential candidate Ulysses Simpson Grant.

Subjective Geography

Modern Primitives

Whether the woman carry a waterpot on her head
deforming her skull; whether her feet
be bound in the cradle to keep
dainty steps from straying; whether the ear lobes
sag with her husband's gold; or her waist contract
to the span of Victorian corsets,
these urges to mutilate ourselves follow us
everywhere. We invoke tribal custom, beauty,
rites of initiation, health and religion
as we torture our bodies, the need
more severe, it is said, among primitives. One
other motive remains: to punish,
and what more efficient than asking the law-
breaker to punish herself?

When my father made a
fist of his firm right hand, flexing
his muscle, the small tattoo
ballooned to a legend—C. C. Defrees—scrolled in
blue on his upper arm. It didn't say
Notary Public, but it could have. Oh he was a
marked (and remarkable) man! Our fingers
traced the salmon-colored border. Daddy, do it
again! The man who ordered that
modest tattoo wasn't the soft-spoken father
we knew, though he could be
reckless with nickels at the slot machines
in the bus depot.

Dusting her nose with a powder
puff, my mother quoted Sir John Davies
whom she hadn't heard of: *Beauty's only skin-deep*.
At the time, she was opposed to
the hard stuff: rouge, lipstick, mascara.
Worst of all, hair-dye, the work of the devil, no
daughter of hers, *et cetera*.
When I was stubborn—that is, almost always—my
father said, *She's hard-headed, she was brought up
on goat's milk*. In contests with my sister
I proved it again and again,
banging my skull with books, almost
to concussion.

Years later, the eye-doctor said,
You have a fixed pupil. What happened?
I couldn't recall. *Never a dull
blow to the head?* In the convent, an eager pupil,
I studied the lives of saints
who walked with pebbles in their shoes,
wore hair-shirts and crowns
of thorn. Deathless lines in my head, I limped
along, born to two noble callings.
Even now—at large and briefly immortal—I flog
myself with gilt-tipped
scourges, lie on a bed of rushes, vowed to be
better than good.

The Giraffe Women of Burma

Their voices reach us as if from the shaft
of a well, these long-necked
women of Padaung, whose clavicles, depressed
by all that brass, reveal
the burden of beauty. Over the miles, the years,
I shoulder the weight, embrace the wood
of our common cross, and under the load,
the scars, these bold
striations.

       Slung from my neck, the brass-bordered
crucifix like the ring on my hand
recalled an earlier day when priest and medicine man
shaped the first coil for the five-year-old
with fiery promise and a flash of metal. Then:
divination with relics, with chicken bones
for the favored time. Protection from tiger bites,
one legend says, and I feel the stripes
change subtly

       as elders rehearse the punishment
for adultery. The necklace of habit removed,
atrophied muscles let go
and the light-headed woman surrenders her weight
to a coffin. Meanwhile, these ringing
tiers and silver chains, coins
swung from the links, tell the world
who these women are, identify their tribe. Legs
shackled with brass

or held in place by detailed
prescriptions, reduce their walk
to a hobble. The pillow under the chin does not
spell comfort, but elegance
in position. They cannot tilt the head back
to drink sweet water, must bow to sip
from a straw. If they set their ornaments aside,
against the tribal law, they need
a brace or the hand of a friend, merely
to keep on breathing.

            In a Rangoon hospital, X-rays
screen the skeletal change: collarbone
shoved down, ribs displaced, a neck
that, year by year, looks
longer. The downward pressure on the spine
means something has to give. All through the blank
December I chose unfrocking, my one
alternative, I held my head carefully
above the collar,

            folded the turtle-neck twice
in a mockery of survival. My lungs filled
with water, closing. Whatever raises this voice
from a long way down
lies close to you as air. Help me to hold up my head.

Women of the Veil

The veils that hide us are everywhere one.
Our glories must be guarded by a screen
to shield a lovely secret from the sun.

It's harder every day to keep us clean
when female Bedouins are looking out for more.
Hard edges soften in the evergreen

surround of forest haze and foggy shore.
Too strict attention stones a woman's gift.
The mist looked through we know as metaphor.

Saharan Nomads

Like the bedouin cooking his dinner
astride a camel, I knew mine was a
movable feast. The joys of religious
observance were tempered by bad
traveler's luck. Never much of a nomad,
even less of a cook, I counted on God
and the Blessed Mother to help me
over the hump. I pitched my tent near
the notice board, eternally vigilant
in my zeal for marching orders.
Tried to remain at the ready, dorm
windows clear as a prophet,
floor waxed, everything packed but my
nightgown and toothbrush.

No, that's a lie, though it's true
I tried. That's the efficient soul I
roomed next to, who followed the Way of
the Cross at 5:20, minutes after
rising, said the rosary before others
had dressed for morning prayer.
No wonder she polished the floor a week
ahead, dwelling like birds of the air who
sleep with their clothes on. Time after
time, waiting for the mop,
in line for the vacuum, hand on smooth
handle, the bell called me
to chapel, to a meal prepared in
the convent kitchen.

Now when it's time to travel, I travel
that 30-year gulf to meet the divided
self schooled by the Desert
Fathers. Turban and veil, I am still
riding the Greyhound bus, tonight
the Empire Builder—mountain-
terrain on a pass—somebody else's
signature. I am Sister
Mary Companion, must copy the missing
person's name. The conductor
jokes that Sister Monica must be a Berber
using his train for a shuttle. He says
I've grown thin overnight.

My throat feels dry. Lost in the glare
of another departure, I veer
into sand, into wind, eager to bury myself
in *The Wasteland*. Something fatal
comes on—I'm not certain what (past
accident, plot)—uncontrollably burning.

Nest Gatherers of Tiger Cave, Thailand

Wherever the swiftlets fly, we follow. Two miles
into the cave the slow drops
coalesce into icicle forms—yellow-brown, milky,
gray, the dark green of
black-opal. We lash bamboo with vines to centuries-
old stalactites for the barefoot
climb. Nothing but skill to break our fall, we
keep on climbing.

            Torch in the teeth, up, up, 300
feet towards the porcelain
gleam of *white gold,* the nests of dried
bird saliva, we press on to the far
rock face. Generations of climbers. Beyond the brush
of wing against cheek, the twittering
call of white birds and black,

                 we work 10 hours a day,
come back to the cave mouth over the sea. At rest
on the bamboo platform, we eat fish for dinner,
watch TV, and wait for Mr. Apichat,
the collector, to call on his tour of 60 islands.
He will buy the nests. He will bring a new
battery. Next week, in Hong Kong, some man from
another world will order Bird's Nest Soup.

The Tuareg Smith

Working a silver padlock the size of a
thumbnail, the Tuareg smith says,
That's our life! Ant, hyena and jackal
appear with a stylized sun, the horse's
hoof, the fickle stars, moon and a woman
he loves. Laughter greets the good
silver eye under the devil's eyebrows.
Call him drifter and scoundrel,
the smith keeps his design
classic by moving forever on. Where he
camps for a day, he executes the bad
taste of his neighbors.

The nun belonged to a tribe almost as
wary of gold as her African
brother. Except for the crown of a tooth
blessed with permission
her track followed the way of the snail
stencilled in silver. To give the devil
his due, the silver trim
of her Eversharp and fountain pen
proclaimed the hymn she swayed to
as surely as the elaborate
habit and the Little Office book
she chanted from.

The smith recognized gold for an evil
omen. His hand—or anyone's—
ringed in such luxury was bound to be
turned aside by the Prophet.
There the nun parted company with
the silversmith. She treasured the gold
band of her heavenly marriage.

The ringed right hand clasped to its
partner marked her a Bride of Christ.
She loved the smooth feel of gold
against skin, initials of the
Holy Family engraved within.

The smith worked in metal. The nun
with needle and thread. Each pleat of
the coif, every linen tuck
warded off imperfection, said that she
cared enough to obey in trivial
matters the letter that kills. And it
killed her. Tied her in knots
neither hand nor attentive ear
could undo, the detail
finer than filigree, shot through with
the intricate silver of silence.

The woman inside the vanished nun trains
her eyes on the jewelry counter,
celebrates life given back in the sixth
decade. Wrist and ear heavy with
silver, a lover returns to the golden
word: to letters eroded on the slender
band round the little finger of her
writing hand. In the ninth lame hour
she hears again: *Silver and gold
have I none.* And lame from the womb, she
rises up at the temple gate
that is called Beautiful, where such as
they have they give.

Honey Hunters of Nepal

These are big game bees. When I'm after something
sweet I want to make the most of it. Thousands of
miles from Nepal, I'm on the level
summer deck behind my house. It's happy hour. I'm
wearing nasturtium colors, oleander
perfume, powder. Seductive as a flower, I study
the wings on my wineglass. I am
haloed with bees and beatitudes.

Nine hunters of honey in Nepal, Mani Lal their head.
This afternoon I'd gladly join them. I know
how to cling to the cliffside, avert my eyes from the
dizzying drop. I can pray. Here and now, I reap
the harvest from years of religious
modesty, countenance serene as a china plate. Draped
in a veil of drones, queens and workers,
I am high on experience in attic apartments where

wasps and urban yellow jackets swarm under the eaves
every spring. Imaginary beekeeper,
I will not be checked by the actual, will hold onto
my thin rope more surely than Sylvia Plath.
Step, step, bamboo! setting my foot on the fiber
ladder like Jacob's dream angels, ascending,
descending. These flights of euphoria visit me rarely
now that I'm older than Mani Lal.

The honeybees I choose—*Apis laboriosa*, the world's
largest—must create a legend to equal
the story of Ambrose: a swarm from the brood comb
settled on my mouth as I lay in my cradle, the omen
propitious. It was raining honey.
Here lies the honey-tongued Hillsboro poet! What if
the bees make me suffer at times. I tweeze
the stingers from arms and legs, keeping my eyes on

Mani Lal, lips chanting my mantras. He carries a
bamboo basket lined with wild goatskin.
I would take my skin from the goat my father bought.
Her milk recovered my life from the foxglove of
formula. Here is her snapshot in the family album.

Illuminations

Emily Dickinson and Gerard Manley Hopkins

My notebook shows they took a formal cruise,
floated past bridges in the morning light.
From cliffs of fall to mid-Atlantic blues
they traveled fifteen knots the day her White
Election fell to his Ignatian news
of still pastures and feel-of-primrose night.
I owe my life to that New England nun
and triple locks the musing lover sprung.

In Amherst Emily prepared to risk it:
she scrawled some verse on napkins, tucked the wild
game in the hamper, doubled a batch of biscuit
dough and stepped over her father's threshold
while the old man napped. Too timorous to ask it
—he may have dreamed her docile as a child—
Gerard approved, leaving his Company behind
for her improbable liquor, out of his mind.

The world they charged led soon to a famous wreck;
both saw it looming off the coast of Wales.
The demure velvet ribbon about her neck
was not a leash, and cautionary tales
rang true. Her cries rose with the waves on deck,
the lioness again, breasting the gales
that left her adamant to write the letter
granting each heart its stone for worse or better.

The first three drafts were bitter as dark beer.
The next seemed overlong; the fifth, too frantic.
She made a couplet timed to disappear
the instant one considered it pedantic
and for the stricken lute of the sonneteer
a veiled refrain of grief become romantic.
Not one would do. She'd have to write in bed.
He found her there and straightway lost his head.

She showed Gerard where he would find his own
pale eyes inside the velvet-tethered locket.
Poor Emily! How else could she have known
he carried Whitman in his greatcoat pocket?
It's best, I think, to leave the pair alone
until their dull dough sours on the captain's docket.
In any case there's no communion service
when this bread's gone and Emily is nervous.

How could she give him up to any storm
after the voyage shared—those breathless dashes—
a line all stress, or nearly so, a form
impervious as slag, set free of ashes.
Let others rest in harbor, safe and warm.
They found their comfort in the cold sea crashes
the black west sent to beat the soldier's cave;
that Roman collar carried to the grave,

laid like a wreath over the unmarked vault
where bones of ghostly lovers washed ashore
on her white beach. The sand ground from basalt
by wind and wave in the skull's unquiet roar
was soft-sift now, though powerless to halt
the glassed descent from ecstasy and more.
These brief affairs we label mid-Victorian,
seduce the timid soul of wit's historian.

"Gerard," Emily wrote, under a sky all sunset,
"It's over—like a tune—the sad Campaign
of Sting and Sweet—will never be the one let
soar—The Auctioneer of Parting—bid the rain
rehearse the dew." Her pen assailed the runlet
crossing the intimate sheet with a purple stain,
my Grandmother Dickinson, dyed in the clerical woof,
was warped for good. I am the living proof.

Ernst Barlach

Frost and Hunger. Your stolen title, the one thing left,
my Massachusetts weekly
check after taxes. It picks up a poet's
phrase for our time in Montana, a nice
security gone to hell.

                    Barlach said, For everything—
paradise, hell, one disguised as the other—there is
expressive form. He knew them all, last
of the realist sculptors. Cold fell. On Russian
steppes, knives turned
savage in the gut.

                He set Slavic bone against the wind.
The laughing man laughed still, the sad
musician played. A solid peasant swirled his cape
before the swordsman wind. The rest is never
mind. In the end, a frieze of listeners
carved from missing hearts.

                    Intruder here, brash
westerner, footprints too recent,
thin on old New England rock, I pull on boots, my cupboard
bare, and look to Barlach for relief. "At bottom,
that's what we are—beggars, problem characters. In the Slav,
it shines out while others hide it."

                    The hidden
body of this waiting curves around waiting
forms, assumes the shape of a cup
extended. I beg sorrow to fill it up, flare like a bell,
ring the dissolution of the veil, hands
not knowing themselves
numb on the great bronze clapper.

Eminent Victorians

Those years I hated them meant simply: I did not
love my chains. The click of rosary beads,
black olives around the waist,
made straight the way of strait-laced Sister Victoria
patrolling classroom aisles. Sometimes
as she bent to guide my pencil, I could surprise
a glimpse of neck under the shirtfront starch,
her guimpe's white circle
standing away from the body.

                      I'd see myself
floating on billowy skirts, far from land's familiar.
Joining hands in the wrong order, I kept
my beads in vast pockets of unholy things: man-sized
linen handkerchiefs, scourge of envelope verses,
silk-lined purse for white veil pins
and thread. I learned to chant the Office of the Dead
in smooth Latin and detested those grotesque
small sinners Dickens sentimentalized.

                      Remembered
Twist at ten: a cautionary orphan's story
I insisted suffering to the end
because I'd checked it out. In high school
I panned the thick fog of *Two Cities:*
Madame Defarge knitting away the French Revolution.

65

Would she send mittens and scarves like Grandma?
Recalling evidence of devotion,
I admitted Dickens' worldly wit
and made my first concession:

                              Charles, we are all
in your debt, in your debtors' prison: writing
our lives, installments of a flight
pure as Jesus' walk on water. What matter
that the world is evil if our words contain it?
I watch the Seven Swords of Mary's sorrow
pierce Victoria's heart, spiked bouquet in a holy
frog, and marvel at the red
stain on the starched forehead, sign that Jesus
wants to share His crown.

                              I plan to carry mine,
the veils and crosses, oil in my lamp: a ready Bride
on time for the Wedding Feast. Far from London's
seamy side, the one Dickens penetrated, I would
remain aloof, my legendary
life. I keep my eye on the models: cool as Jesus,
holy Bread in the tabernacle
I believed an icebox: Father, watch your priestly
hand—frostbite more dangerous than fire.

Greta Garbo and the Star Messenger

Her face the preface to water, stirred.
The least ripple widens out to the rim.
Minnows flicker up from the still bottom,
fins unwinding a silver discord.
Nothing is said. The arrested word
fades under indolent cloud. A faint drum
throbs in the temple's delirium
and disappears like the flight of a bird.

Alone in theatric dark, I feel her mood
inscribe the face I turn to the silver screen.
Secret lovers, rivers of solitude
and a heaven of fixed stars maroon
the woman we know. On the island a reed
bends into the current and is gone.

Marianne Moore

Marianne Moore, did you wear the tricorne
hat into that heaven of animals
evolved from your careful pen? You are
the one who said, "Fashion can make you
ridiculous; style . . . attractive—a near
siren." Over the white-capped
wake, I examine your favorite, "a black
satin-straw [in the wind] sailor
with narrow moiré ribbon tied to the side
overlapping the nibs of crow feathers
laid in a fan around the brim."

Now that's quite a hat and might overcome
my fear of torture brought on as a
child with oversized head and a millinery
mother who sided with Paul on Sundays.
My crowning glory at 10, a Buster Brown cut,
would have been right with a halo,
but Mother drove saleswomen to superhuman
fits of fitting. Could they have learned
to admire your sentence: "That man is
freckled like a trout with
impropriety"? Heading for the stockroom

they'd say, "We specialize in large sizes."
If my mother's grammar was poor, in moral
and biblical matters, she was
stricter than yours. Nothing too soft would
soothe her. Nothing with stretch
would do: hat after hat, too old for my
years—Holbein, perhaps, four

centuries later—or too small in spite of
desperate measures. "No problem, we'll
size it." Again and again, they'd loosen
the ribbon, place the hat on the block,

expand the abstract head where the felt life
grew distorted. Little wonder Sundays
were one continuous headache. Did I become
addicted to pain, put on the linen
bandeau and coif, the name a martyr's crown
stiffened to perfection that came off
only in secret? Starch set a crease in my
forehead. Starch scaled my vision
down. My hat's off to Elizabeth Bishop, who
called you "innately flirtatious." You
were courageous as well, learning

to drive at 70. Dead or alive I tackled
the wheel at 50 and still consider
that move miraculous. Maybe I'll take to hats
in 20 years, but I doubt it. Berets
perhaps or a peasant scarf, too much like a
veil in chill weather. Your impulse unveiled
in Bishop drives me: "The exact way . . . anything
was done, or made, or functioned was poetry"
to you. I'm grateful for that, as for
"an element of mortal panic . . . underlying all
works of art," again according to Bishop,

whose efforts of affection may be the best
we can hope for, apart from your poems
and prose that refuses indulgence. The crow,
a two-syllable experiment, led you
to fantasize "Pluto, the true Plato," with pro-
pensities I admire from a distance: for rings,
gold thimbles and gems; buckwheat cakes,
fruits of all kinds, watercress, dehydrated
alfalfa. Where the lion lies down
with the lamb, may you come to the final
reward of precision, beyond the "Triple Crown"

of the Bollingen, the National Book Award, and
the Pulitzer. May the beasts you admired
in print, in the circus, re-invent themselves,
arriving under perfect control in their full
animal vitality. And may we gather the jewels
with the lessons, secure in our theft,
born of impeccable taste, like your unacknowledged
take-over of a phrase from your student,
E*liz*abeth: "the bell-boy with the buoy-balls."
"Perhaps we are all magpies," Elizabeth
says, if only on the gallows.

Maria Callas, the Woman Behind the Legend*

Her biographer gives us the woman, the artist:
two sides of a coin presenting
contrary faces. She calls the woman *Maria,*
the artist *La Callas,* a Greek
bearing gifts to Milan, darling and scourge of
La Scala and not to be trusted. When hecklers
tossed radishes onto the stage
La Callas smiled, ecstatic, gathered them to
her breast like the loveliest

                            roses. In her
fifties Maria asked, *Why doesn't anyone write
an opera for Mary Magdalene?* That
vision of washing a god's feet with her tears:
what convincing drama! I could have been
useful there: I carried my mother's genes for
histrionics, tear-ducts the most active
prop in my repertoire. Cried—not just from
remorse, depression and worse. I cried
from relief, anger,

                          sudden noise, the exact
turn of a phrase, the terrors and joys
of total understanding. And drying the savior's
feet with my hair: the image obsessed me,
though my skimpy locks had been

* Title from biography by Arianna Stassinopoulos

71

chopped off at three in hopes that short hair
would thicken. All over town, my sister's
luxuriant curls spilled from studio windows on
both sides of the block.

      Maria, the man I've
found, man I will never marry,
calls me *La Maddalena*. My hair on the cutting-
room floor nearly white, it was
late luck invited him in. The art each of us
lives by, a country between us, keeps us
apart. Two faces of one coin at the going rate,
obverse joining reverse, close
to the other side.

George Eliot (Mary Ann Evans Cross)

She has . . . cultivated every art to make herself attractive,
feeling bitterly . . . what a struggle it was, without beauty,
whose influence she exaggerates as do all ugly people.

LADY JEBB

Lost in her stories' complex flow, I drowned
the sorrows of adolescence, worked
through a reading list from my favorite
history teacher. The writer's life promised
more. Somewhere there had to exist
a man in love with a woman whose gift was the
mind alone. This is how I began
the solitary life, apart from domestic duties,
absent from mealtime chatter.

                       My idol preferred
subdued colors, hoping to fade into the
tasteful décor of the drawing-room. Married or
not, no matter, her passionate
mind cut a swath through intellectual circles.
You would perhaps have been amused,
she writes, *to see an affectionate . . . dowdy
friend splendid in grey moiré
antique—the consequence of a . . . lecture from
Owen Jones.*

                    If the long-banished nun sneaks into
my dressing-room mirror, into my
worst recurrent nightmare—the one with familiar

strangers proclaiming the common
life—I cross myself with Sister Margaret Jean
whose stroke or heart attack jangled the intricate
circuitry of her language. She
fought back, made her painful way to the fifth-
grade reader, checked out

                     with the switchboard
humming. Today I lift my receiver
to keep the important calls coming. Thanks to two
marginal women, I still have the word, the world
listening in.

About the Author

Madeline DeFrees was born in Oregon in 1919. After graduating from high school at sixteen, she entered the Sisters of the Holy Names of Jesus and Mary, where she was known for many years as Sister Mary Gilbert. She received a B.A. degree from Marylhurst College in 1948 and an M.A. degree from the University of Oregon in 1951.

For many years she taught at Oregon and Washington schools of the order, at Holy Names College, Gonzaga University, Marylhurst College, the University of Washington, the University of Victoria, and the University of Montana. After receiving a dispensation from her religious vows in 1973, she went on to direct the creative writing program at the University of Massachusetts and retired in 1985.

DeFrees is highly regarded as a writer, scholar, and teacher. She continues to serve on various judging panels, gives readings of her work, and leads workshops in both poetry and prose across the country. She currently lives in Seattle, Washington.

Design by Ken Sánchez.

Text set in Sabon by G & S Typesetters, Inc., Austin, Texas.

Printed on acid-free paper and Smyth sewn
by Malloy Lithographing, Inc., Ann Arbor, Michigan.